Words and Pictures by

Elizabeth O. Dulemba

For Stan (always),
Olivia and Hugh.

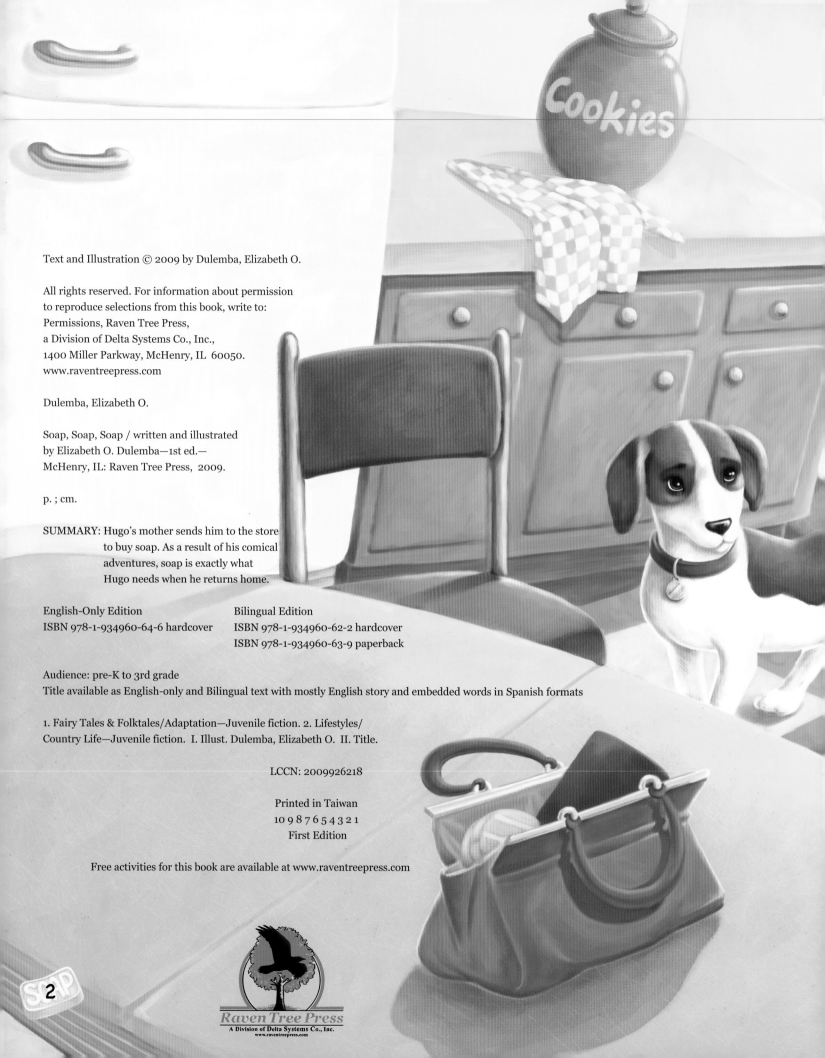

Dulemba, Elizabeth O.

Soap, Soap, Soap / written and illustrated
by Elizabeth O. Dulemba—1st ed.—
McHenry, IL: Raven Tree Press, 2009.

p. ; cm.

SUMMARY: Hugo's mother sends him to the store
to buy soap. As a result of his comical
adventures, soap is exactly what
Hugo needs when he returns home.

English-Only Edition
ISBN 978-1-934960-64-6 hardcover

Bilingual Edition
ISBN 978-1-934960-62-2 hardcover
ISBN 978-1-934960-63-9 paperback

Audience: pre-K to 3rd grade
Title available as English-only and Bilingual text with mostly English story and embedded words in Spanish formats

1. Fairy Tales & Folktales/Adaptation—Juvenile fiction. 2. Lifestyles/
Country Life—Juvenile fiction. I. Illust. Dulemba, Elizabeth O. II. Title.

LCCN: 2009926218

Printed in Taiwan
10 9 8 7 6 5 4 3 2 1
First Edition

Free activities for this book are available at www.raventreepress.com

Raven Tree Press
A Division of Delta Systems Co., Inc.
www.raventreepress.com

"Hugo, please run to the store
for me," his mother said and
handed him some money.
"Go straight to the store
and buy soap."

But Hugo's path to the store was
across the playground,
down the sidewalk,
and beyond the ditch
that ran by Hugo's school.
Hugo wanted to remember what he needed
to buy, so all the way to the store he said,
"soap, soap, soap!"

Hugo was near the playground when he slipped in a puddle of mud.

Kersploosh!

His slide through the mud surprised Hugo so much that he forgot what his mother wanted him to buy at the store.

Hugo stood frowning at the mud puddle.

He walked to the left of the puddle. "Here I remembered."

He walked to the right. "There I forgot."

Just then Hugo's neighbor, Jellybean Jones, walked by. She said, "If you tell me what you're looking for, I'll help you find it."

"I don't know!" Hugo replied.
"Here I remembered.
There I forgot."

"You're a funny boy, Hugo. And muddy too!"
Jellybean said as she hurried by. And then . . .

Jellybean slipped in the mud puddle too.

Kersploosh!

"Whoa," she said. "The mud is as slippery as soap!"
Suddenly Hugo remembered and shouted "soap!"

Jellybean yelled, "Now I'm muddy
too and it's your fault!"
"I'm sorry," Hugo said as he ran away.
But then he had "I'm sorry" stuck in his
head and forgot all about the soap.

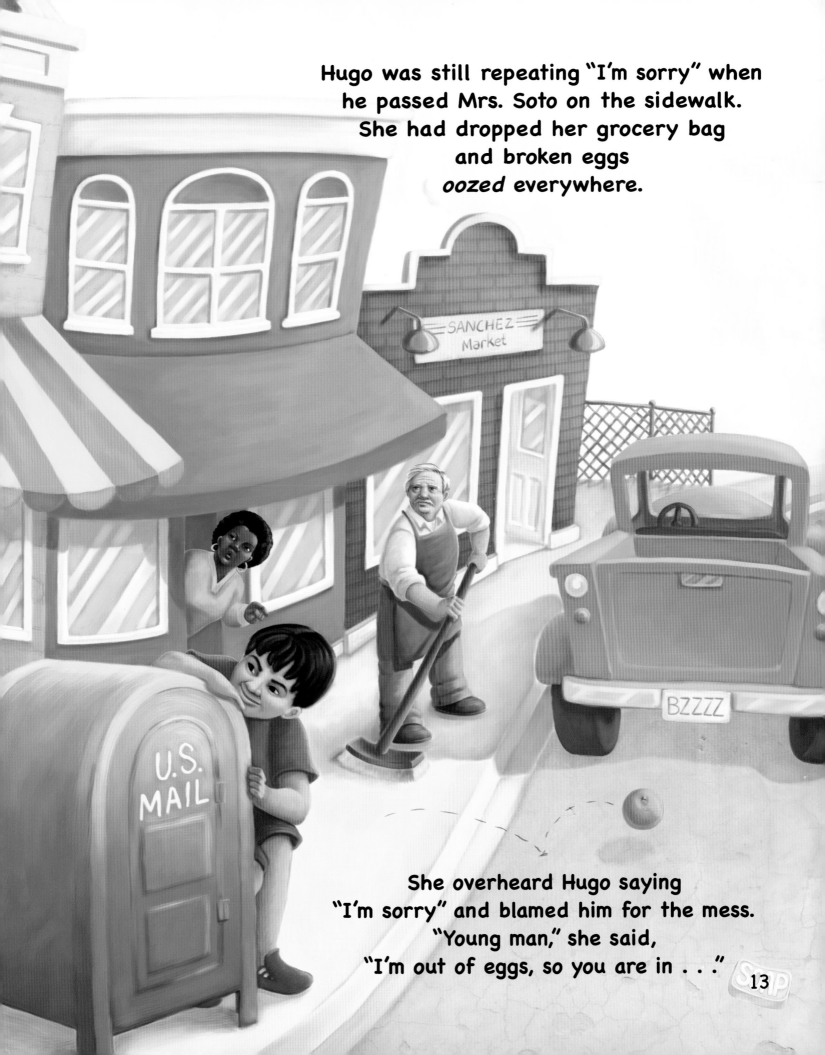

Hugo was still repeating "I'm sorry" when
he passed Mrs. Soto on the sidewalk.
She had dropped her grocery bag
and broken eggs
oozed everywhere.

She overheard Hugo saying
"I'm sorry" and blamed him for the mess.
"Young man," she said,
"I'm out of eggs, so you are in . . ."

Hugo didn't hear the rest.
He wriggled free and took off running.
But now he had "I'm out, so you are in"
stuck in his head.
And he still could not remember what
his mother wanted him to buy at the store.

Hugo started to jump over the ditch that ran by his school. He didn't see Bubba down in the muck. But the bully heard Hugo say, "I'm out, so you are in."

Bubba yelled, "I'll show you who's in!" and pulled Hugo into the ditch.

Just then Principal Vargas arrived on the scene.
"Stop! Break this up!" he said and sent Bubba home.
"My goodness! Hugo, you are a mess.
You need a bath with lots of soap!"
Suddenly Hugo remembered and shouted "soap!"

Now Hugo was muddy *and* stinky too,
but he still had to go to the store.
To help him remember what he
needed to buy, Hugo kept repeating

Soap! Soap! Soap!

Mr. Sanchez, the grocer, said,
"Oh, Hugo, what would you like?"
Hugo smiled and said, "soap, soap, soap!"
"Of course!" Mr. Sanchez said.

Hugo handed Mr. Sanchez his
money and finally got the soap.
"Thank you!" Hugo said as he ran out
the door and back toward his home.

This time he
jumped over
the ditch.

He dodged around
Mrs. Soto who was
still complaining
about her eggs.

And he hurried across the playground—
except near the mud puddle.
There he walked very, very slowly.

When Hugo returned home, his mother was
happy to see him—but not the mud.
"My goodness!" she cried.
"Hugo, you're a mess! You need a bath.
It's no wonder we use so much soap!"

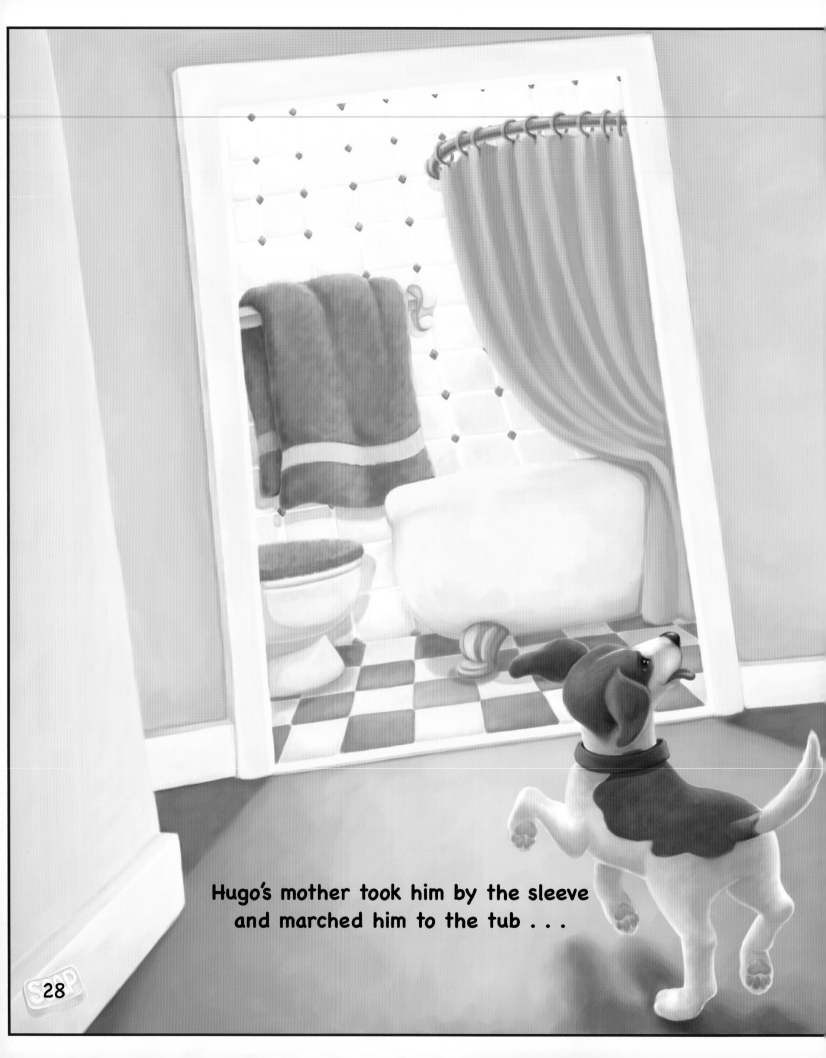

Hugo's mother took him by the sleeve
and marched him to the tub . . .

. . . where she made him scrub, scrub, scrub with the soap, soap, soap!

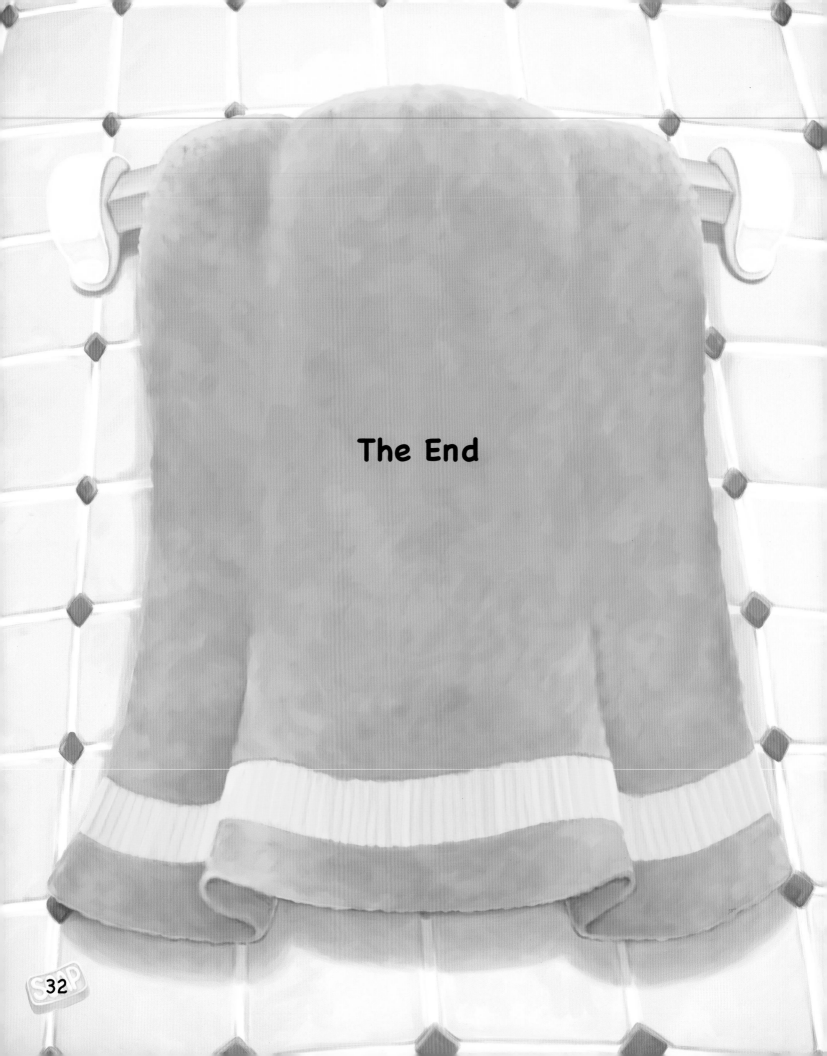

The End